This Makes Me Jealous

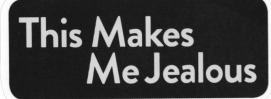

This Makes Me JEALOUS

RODALE KiDS

This Makes Me Jealous

Courtney Carbone
Illustrated by Hilli Kushnir

For anyone who needs a friend, that they may be a friend —C.C.

To Liam and Aya, my team of bandits and partners-in-crime —H.K.

Text copyright © 2019 by Courtney Carbone
Cover art and interior illustrations copyright © 2019 by Hilli Kushnir

All rights reserved. Published in the United States by Rodale Kids,
an imprint of Random House Children's Books, a division of Penguin Random House LLC, New York.

Rodale and the colophon are registered trademarks of Penguin Random House LLC.

Visit us on the Web! rhcbooks.com

Educators and librarians, for a variety of teaching tools, visit us at RHTeachersLibrarians.com

Library of Congress Cataloging-in-Publication Data is available upon request.
LCCN 2018011829 (print) | LCCN 2018018245 (ebook) | ISBN 978-1-63565-078-5 (trade) | ISBN 978-1-63565-077-8 (pbk.) |
ISBN 978-1-63565-082-2 (ebook)

MANUFACTURED IN CHINA   10 9 8 7 6 5 4 3 2   First Edition

Random House Children's Books supports the First Amendment and celebrates the right to read.

RODALE
KiDS

A new girl named Amy came to school today.

She walked in
during my show-and-tell!

Everyone ignored me
and stared at her.

4

I felt as prickly
as my cactus plant.

My teacher asked me
to share my desk.

I did not like having to share my things.

7

The other kids crowded
around Amy at recess.

I did not see
what the big deal was.

Next we played soccer in gym class.

It was my turn
to be the goalie.

But Amy made me
look bad.

She scored a goal
on her very first kick.

Hooray!
Everyone cheered.

I felt like the ball
hit me in the stomach.

I stomped off the field.

My teacher stopped me.
She asked what was wrong.

17

I thought about my day.
I thought about Amy.

How was I feeling?
I was feeling JEALOUS.

My teacher listened.
She nodded.

She then asked me how *Amy* must feel.

I had not thought
about how Amy felt.
It must be hard
to be the new kid.

My teacher asked me
what I could do to help.

I said I would try
to be a friend to Amy.

I found Amy
near our desk.

I shared my paints.
We started to talk.

Soon we were laughing and having fun.

I barely noticed
when the bell rang!

I am glad I gave
Amy a chance.

I think we will be
good friends after all.

Today I was jealous.
What makes YOU jealous?

This Makes
Me Jealous

This Makes Me
JEALOUS

RODALE
KiDS